The Book of the Dead
by
Stanley Alexander Martin

Copyright 2007 Nana baBa jaH-aYe
ISBN: 978-0-9559904-1-0

Dedicated to all who **believe**….

A version of this book was first printed in "Death of the God", 2001 sponsored by Mind, and The Millennium Commision....

"0":   Form contents mythics
(after Raymond Williams)

1:   Content forms mythics
(after Vladimir Propp)

0 : Equilibrium
1 : dis-Equilibrium
2 : Search
3 : re-Equilibrium
4 : Wedding

(Innocence "Before")
(i)
(he hid the nakedness from Him because he was "Aware")
(he kneweth "his nakedness" with Him because he was "conscious")
:~   ("I")

2:   Part One   Premonition of Death

I.	Kyrie	-	Fell/risen
II.	Gloria	-	Cursed/praised
III.	Credo	-	Dismissed
IV.	Sanctus	-	Made sacred/profane
V.	Benedictus	-	Blessed/turned
VI.	Agnus Dei	-	Sacrificed

3:   Part Two   The Plagues

4:   Part Three   Exodus

       I.   The Radlett Road
       II.   Radlett to St. Pancreas
       III.   The split Red Sea
       IV.   King's Cross to Acton Town
       V.   Acton Town: The Five Commandments

5:   The Promised Land

1: Content forms mythics
*(after
Sigmund Freud
Ferdinand de Saussure
Vladimir Propp
Claude Levi-Strauss
Noam Chomsky
Roland Barthes
Raymond Williams
Jacques Lacan
Jacques Derrida)*

1. neUn maths
0. *(Theses)* **Premises - Doings**

1. "0" ~ (1 x "0") = utterance of nothingness = a real : God's Word
2. "0" : "1" ~ = 1 &... = a real
3. 1 &... : "2" ~ = 2 &... = a real

I. *(Anti-theses)* **Theses - Actions**

1. "0" ~ utterance of nothingness = real ~ WORD ~ Thoth/Nu ~ God

2. "i" ~ fourth root of 1 = real

3. "i^2" ~ root 1 ~ = -1 = real

4. "i^3" ~ -i ~ fourth root of 1 = real

5. "i^4" ~ "1" ~ = 1 = real

6. "pi" ~ 3 + j = approx. 3.1415926 = real

7. "1" ~ = 1^0 = 1 = real

8. 1 + 1 ~ = 2^1 = 2 = real

9. 1 x 1 ~ = 2^0 ~ = 2 = 1 = real

II. (Syntheses - Dialectics) "Lies" - Works/plays

1.   "0"   ~   approx. 0.83

2.   "i"   ~   1/(root 2)

3.   "i^2"   ~   1/2

4.   "i^3"   ~   1/2(root 2)

5.   "i^4"   ~   "1"   =   1

6..   pi   ~   3 + j = approx. 3.1415926

7.   "1"   ~   "2"   ~ = 2

8@9.   (1 + 1)/(1 x 1) : (1 x 1)(1 x 1) : & ~ "2" : ***Too*** ~ = 2 ~ = 8+ : ***river*** ~ = 4 : 4 :   *...for*

III.   (Happenings) "Truths" - Happenings

"0" : Equilibrium

At Birth/Death, Osiris Ra, The River, is at Flood… He glimses "Eternity"….

1 : dis-Equilibrium

He, the Rising Sun, glimpses the sufferings/madness of His "Life"….

2 : Search

The Risen Sun begins to explore the contradictions of His "Path"….

3 : re-Equilibrium

aBraxas, "Fullness" is obtained…. Osiris Ra ascends into (the) Morning….

4 : Wedding

At "Eternity", in aBraxas, "still", the gOd nourishes/is nourished…..

IV. (*Demo*) "Myths" - Demonstrations

Content "for" Mythics
(after Claude Levi-Strauss:Greek myths are structures of how to form "2" from "1")

(f-o-r = from/"f-o-r-m" = dark sign "o" present/move)

i.

Strauss' *Greek Myths* F (x) : F (y) ~ F (y): F (B)
                                    a   b   a   -x

Reappraisal Greek Myths: $A = F$ (x) : F (y) ~ $B = F$ (b): F (Y)
                              $a = -(i^2):i^4$ $b = i^2:-(i^4)$ x $a-1$

Translates....   **1/-1:** **-1/1**   ~ **-(1+1/1x1): -2/2:**   **"0"/"0"**

Which translates: "Functions of one and its contradiction, is *transformed* into two, contradicting the Word which is God", eg., contradicting functions Y = -x ; x = -Y......

A man and a woman contradict and are *transformed* into a union of *too* (**light or dark**), in a contradiction with the forces of the WORD which is God...*For example, Adam and Eve in Eden...*

ii.

"Too" Myths: $A = F$ (x) : F (y) ~ **"Too"** = F $(i^2):-(i^4)$: F $(Y)/"1"$
                 $-(i^2):i^4$ $i^2:-(i^4)$ x $-x/i^2$

Which translates: "Functions of One and its contradiction, is *transformed* into two contradicts to it = Too", eg., contradicting functions Y = x + 1; x = Y-1, which yields:

                1/-1 :   **"0"/"0"**   ~ $x^2: i^2/1^2 : 1+1/1x1 : -2 :$ **-2**

A good man contradict with the forces of the WORD and are *transformed* into a union of *too* in a contradiction with another union of *too*... *For example in the Bible when chosen man Adam forms a union with Eve, and their too is contradicted by the too of the field...*

iii.

*iOj Myth*s: $C = F(B = (x^3 + 1)) : F(y^3 -1) \sim$ **River** $= D = F(i^3) : F(y^3 - 1)$
$\qquad\qquad\qquad\quad -i^3 \qquad\qquad i^3 \qquad\qquad\qquad (x^3 + 1) \quad i^3$

Which translates: "Functions of Too and its contradiction, is *transformed* into a discourse of Eight, in a contradicts to the WORD ", eg., contradicting functions :
$Y = x^3 + 1; x = Y^3 - 1$, which yields:

"Too" $= -2 : -B = 2 \quad \sim \quad$ **River** $= 6+2i:8+: \quad i^3 = i^2 = i^3(1-(i^4)) =$ "**0**"

A union of *too* in a contradiction with another union of *too*... are *transformed* into the relay of a discoursive fractal of eight, which contradict the WORD...The Too of Adam and Eve, yielded a discoursive fractal, or *River*, in later tales of Noah, Abraham, Lot, Moses, David, Solomon, Jesus Christ, and Mohammed, and Yogi Singh....

iv.

*one-Self Myth*s: $\sim$ **River** $= D = F(i^3) : F(2 : 1 : 1/2) \sim e = F(i^4) : F(-1)$
$\qquad\qquad\qquad\qquad\quad (1/2 : 1 : 2) \quad i^3 \qquad\qquad\qquad (i^2) \quad\quad (i^4)$

Which translates: "Functions of one-Self and its contradiction, is *transformed* into a discourse of $4 = -4$, in a contradicts to the WORD ", eg., contradicting functions:
$\qquad\qquad\qquad\qquad Y = 2/x = 1/2x; xY = 2 = 2Y$: which
yields:

$\sim \quad$ **River** $= 6+2i:8+: \quad i^3 = i^2 = i^3(1-(i^4)) =$ "**0**" $\sim \mathbf{1/2/4:4:8}$: **(1/2)/1:-1**

A union of *too-River* in a contradiction with another union of *too*... are *transformed* into the relay of a discoursive fractal of four = **"*for*"**, which contradict the WORD... The Too of Adam and Eve, yielded a discoursive fractal, or *River*, in later tales of Noah, Abraham, Lot, Moses, David, Solomon, Jesus Christ, and Mohammed, and Yogi Singh... yielding a modern myth of the ***neUn***:

for : four ~ one : body-trinity : one body/consciousness/spirit/soul...
...neUn ~ one body/consciousness/spirit/soul : one the real/sure/certain/concrete....

Form/content mythics
(after Ferdinand de Saussure)

"for"
Signifiers   -   "0"------------> 1: "Too" :
                 4 : 5!   /
                 3<------------2

Form content mythics
(after Roland Barthes)

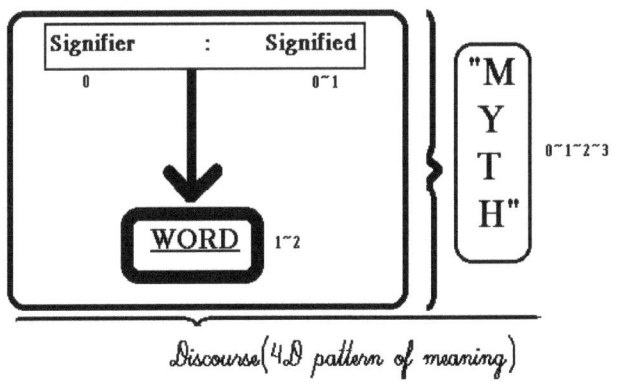

Myth

"0":1-->A *Signifier* refers does at/to the floating utterance of nothingness ("0")...

1:2---> A Signifier always acts as a defers to itself of a *SIGNIFIED*...

2:3---> A *WORD* makes a referral/deferral to A WORK/PLAY OF MEANING, a "lie"...

3:4: The <u>PAROLE</u> of word meanings is relayed (referral/deferral!) in the total language as a "lie-line", a "path to truth", a happening...

4:5:.. Each lie-line is a "<u>MYTH</u>", and owns a pattern of speech, a "<u>DEMO</u>", which is its mythic "truth"...

V. (*Tiers*) **Mythic Discourses - Events**

5:6... PROGRAMMING:

Signifiers -   "0"--------------------> 1: "Too" : "for"
                  4: 5!:6!   /
                  3<----------------------2

    Each "<u>DISCOURSE</u>" owns an program of events, a " TIER", which is its "real" rhetoric.

VI. (*Catastrophes*) **"Sect" - Drama**

6:7. CATALOGUE:

Signifiers -   "0"------------> 1: "Too" : "for"
                  4: 5!:6!:7!   /
                  3<---------------2

    Each "<u>SECT</u>" owns a catalogue of drama, a "CATASTROPHE", which is its "sure" need.

VII. (*Fractals*) **"Cult" - Episodes**

7:8: LIBRARY:

Signifiers -   "0"--------------------> 1: "Too" : "for"
                  4: 5!:6!:7!:8!   /
                  3<----------------------2

    Each "<u>CULT</u>" owns a library of episodes, an EPIC, which is its "certain" greed.

VIII. (*Chaos*) **"Faith" - Incidents**

8:8+: <u>*WEB*</u>....

Signifiers   -   "0"--------------------> 1: "Too" : "for"
                    4:   5!:6!:7!:8!:8+!   /
                    3<-----------------------2

Each "<u>FAITH</u>" owns a web of incidents, a SAGA, which is its concrete mood.

2. Instincts

No genes: *("Lies" - Paths to Truths)*

Form No Categories   *Form Mythic No Categories..................*

IDEAS - Selfish Reader Amino-Acids
(after Jacques Lacan)

```
.----------------Structured 4D----------------     ----------------Structured 8D-------------
-----
---------"0" ~ 1---      --- 1 ~ 2--    ---2 ~ 3--     ---3 ~ 4--                    ---4 ~
5--          ---5 ~ 6 --     ---6 ~ 7 --    ---7 ~ 8--
```

"0" ~ 1   1 ~ 2   2 ~ 3   3 ~ 4   4 ~ 5   5 ~ 6   6 ~ 7   7 ~ 8   8 ~ 8+ = 9

refers	referral	feed	*dial*	*exit*	rise		drift	have	haven
defers	defferal								
refers	protect	guess	know	*conscious*	enlighten		become	ascend	
								transcend	
defers	secrete	connect	link						
signifier		signified		word		parole speech	*rhetoric*	need	greed
									mood
no		no-no	aie	aye	yea	yes	sure	certainly	
								concretely	
un-truth		lay		lie	truth	myth	discourse	sect	cult
									faith
thesis	anti-thesis	synthesis	happening	demo	*tier*	catastrophe	fractal		chaos
impossible	possible	probable	true	myth	*real* *sure*	certain	concrete		
per-	haps	per-haps	happening	demo	event	drama	epic	saga	

no-time   now   past   now-past   now-past-future   *now-future-past* *forever-now*   *eternal-now*
         eternal-forever-now

doing   action   work/play   happening   demo   *event*   drama   episode
                                                             incident

black	red	orange	yellow	green	*blue*		indigo	violet
								psychedelic
abyss	sun	star	sky	heaven	*universe*		abraxa s	diety
								gOd
instincts		body	mind	spirit	soul	*real*	sure	certain
								concrete
anal	oral	sexual	spiritual	soul		*the-real*	*the-sure*	*the-certain* the-concrete
asleep	awake	aware	knowing	conscious	*enlightened*		becoming	ascending
								transcending
refering-	protecting-		thinking-	dream	demonstrate		evene	drama
							episode	create
-defering		-secreting		-connecting-		-linking		
refer	protect	love	adore	possess	*contemplate*	haunt	have	haven defer
	secrete							
pleasure	satisfaction		come	know	own *bliss*		obsess	behave blythe
deny	cause	pretend	tender	conceive	*receive*		bind	pretext text
mortal	living	uttering	dead	living-dead	*deading-dead*	live		live-dead
								immortal

that	what	that-it	that-you	that-You	*that-we*	that-they	that-one
							that, the
who	I	I-thou	I-it	I-We	*I-You*	I-They One	I-The
the	my	mine	me	I	*myself*	the-one I, a	I, the

Machine Coding - Selfless Writer RNA
(after Noam Chomsky)
Deep-structured language

O	Oo	a	ah	awe	*a-awe*	*oo-awe oo-awe awe-awe*
a	ha	aha	aha-ah	aha-aha	*a-a-aha*	*a-a-a-aha a-a-a-a-aha a-a-a-a-aha*
e'	ee	ee-ee	e-e-e	e-e-e-e	*e-e-e-e-e e-e*	*e-e-e-e-e-e e-e-e-e-e- e-e-e-e-e-e-e*
e'	eh	eh-ee	eh-eh	awe	*a-awe*	*oo-awe oo-awe awe-awe*
ma	nana	sah	baas	ra	*ra-rah*	*ra-ra-ra gagah*
fi-mi	fi-yu	fi-s/he/it	fi-wi	fi-you	*fi-dem*	*fi-oonu fi-awe fi-gah*

GENES - Social Programming DNA
(Social discourses, human dimensions)

perfect	same	similar	identical	special	*species*	environment system ecolgy
imperfection	flawed	dis-similar	different		*mutation*	strange alien foreign outside
peace	hearth	home	haven	temple	*cathedral*	tomb sepulchre heaven
crisis	fight	conflict	battle	war	*conflagation*	holocaust apocalypse era
instincts	body	mind	spirit	soul	*real*	sure certain concrete
individual	couple	family	tribe	nation	*people*	world universe heaven
I	thou	s/he/it	us	ours	*people's*	world's Ra's God's
s/he/it/one		couple	family	tribe	nation *people*	world universe heaven
s/he/it	us	ours	We	You	*They*	The-It Ra God
son	father	grand	great	nana	*nenny*	ninny nonny nunny
daughter	mother	grand	great	nana	*nenny*	ninny nonny nunny
son	father	grand	great	nana	*nenny*	saint

					Christ/Buddha/Ram
					angel
son	mother	grand	great	nana	*nenny*
				Madonna Mary/Maya/Sita angel	

Go! Translator

a Oo	=	I am a powerful being
aha	=	I understand
nana a ra	=	My grandmother is a queen
a fi-wi baas	=	This is our ruler
e' eh-eh	=	He/She's actively acting like a high god
e' awe-awe	=	He/She's the biggest type of person

3. Drives to consciousness
(after Sigmund Freud)

Being lusts in "nothingness": a kept vacancy at the roots of "sleep": "*0*":..

One's primary spring is to grow:

contradictions, "i", a drive to to "survive",
an instinct being a to eat and a to drink, being
      a waste to be anal and urinal:
            considerations of "wasting" being a driving instinct:
                  a cry, from a drive often to make/too create from,

contradictions to i, being genital, instincts of sex: to reproduce:
      a desire from need, a drive to create anew,

two both too, both "too" to: creating "I", being : moods of being:
      abouyance: "spurring" you to crisis
      contradicting, *evvayance*: "lacking", making you stop from doing:
"death" instinct:
      deferring to *joyssance*: "blissing", encouraging you to doing,
      contradicting *annewsance*: "pain", stopping doing:
"life" instinct:

all process of I/thou: neGus -sleeping, a kept/vacancy at the start of consciousness
                    neAus -awakening, insight that spurts creation
                    neXus -awareness: thinking, research, translation
                    neYin -ennui, a loss at the feeling of the new/rising
                    neHus -"enlightenment", seeing "anew"...

Lusts being considerations of **bliss**:
                  "*0*": *abouyance*: *evvayance*: *joyssance*:
annewsance:
      anal, a passive response to "feeding", being *oral*
      oral, an active response to "genitality": being *sexual*

passive/active responses:
      sexual, comforting reassurance, a response to "loving", the *spiritual*

spiritual: tempting/tormenting, a response to "adoring", the *soul*
soul: possession, a response to "haunting", the *real*
real: obsession, a response to "contemplating", the *sure*
sure: blessing, a response to "saving/serving", the *certain*
certain: salvationing, a response to "holy-ing", the *concrete*...

this being "holiness" : *lust satisfaction* being a ***blithe***: a programming making a web....

4. neUn consciousness
(synaptical responses)

"0":   neGus :   passivity : stasis : *sleeping* : kept *vacancy* at a beginning...

                                                -------> *refers* - aways
                                                -------> *defers* - allows

"i":   neAus :   activity : conflict : *awakening* : *insights* starting creation...

to
                                                ------> *protecting* - allows

from
                                                ------> *secreting* - allows

"i^2": neXus :   choice : problem : *awareness* ----> thinking : *guessing*
                                                              connecting :

researching

                                                              linking :

translating

<u>   </u>**neYin** :   the loss at *rising to* <u>One</u> leading to *ennuie*, feeling of "new"/boredom ------> a "glip"...

<u>1:</u>   **neHus** : (first *too* quanta) : myth-ing : *lie-ing* : knowing

<u>2:</u>   **neGus-neHus** : (second *too* quanta) : diffrancing : *conscious* : discoursing

<u>3.</u>   **neAus-neHus** : (third *too* quanta) : realising : *enlightened* : programming

<u>4.</u>   **neXus-neHus** : (fourth *too* quanta) : structuring : *sure* : cataloguing

<u>5.</u>   **neHus-neHus** : (fifth *too* quanta) : making true : *certain* : totalising

<u>6.</u>   **neGus-neHus-neHus** : (sixth *too* quanta) : constructing : *concrete* :

    systematising....

5. Go! translating Mythic Alphabet
(after Egyptian heiroglyphics)

a	-	sleeping one/thing/"1"
b	-	be/big
c	-	sighted
d	-	do
e	-	awake one/the spirit in the thing/he, she, it
ee	-	*aware one/consciousness/"I"*
f	-	force/sign dark
g	-	sign light/vehicle
h	-	home/heaven
i	-	aware one/consciousness/"I"
j	-	just/joy
k	-	know
l	-	here
m	-	move
n	-	negatively top/dark chief/black ruler
o	-	connecting one/matter/"0"
oo	-	*linking one/person/"you"*
p	-	take it/leave
q	-	give it/stay
r	-	presently/are
s	-	understanding
t	-	the law/the way/money
u	-	linking one/person/"you"
v	-	two/too
w	-	route
x	-	connecting/suffering
y	-	knowing one/soul/"why"
z	-	end

Letters joining-up add "to" in their middle:
e.g., "oo" = "connecting one to connecting one"
 = "**one** connecting one"
 = "linking one".
Letters join-up to make words,
e.g., "book" = "be to linking one to know"
 = "be you know"
"The Book of the Dead" means:
"the way e be you know connecting one to force the Way e a do"....

Knowledge

a	e	I	O	u	y	"iou"	"iously"	sure
dreamt	*protected*		*thought/aware*		*connected*		*linked*	*known*
	conscious	*enlightened*	*become*					
	secreted							
sleeping	waking	aware	aware aware		knowing		conscious	enlightening
become								

6.   one-Self
(after Standard English)

Word knows excellence of *no*-thing in all *things, body, one*: the tribute of the River;

Something, Somebody, Someone holds the keys:
Anything, Anybody, Anyone can the further stairs, and scent the Heaven sent;
Everyting, Everybody, Everyone has the dream:
All-of-one: body: thing knows

gOd: *God* is almighty;

Here a *Person body* speaks

To *Child*: is

Unborn to

The *Spirit* awakening...

Love is the inner winding chords to *Too*: *soul*:

and, Love is *for*: the *Real, Sure, Certain*: *Concrete*....

7. Intro to duB-poetry

The term *duB-poetry*, meaning "poetry with a musical rhythm", usually reggae rhythms, was coined in the 1970's by duB-poet. Oku Onoura; the genre had already been explored by ohn Cooper Clarke, and Linton Kwesi Johnson in Britain and others in Jamaica.

Some of the roots of duB-poetry lies in the Jamaican dj's like I-Roy and Big Youth, and comes from a tradition of poetry set to music harking back to the Last Poets, in the United States, and Beat Poets in the 1950's and 1960's. As a form, duB-poetry is a survival through slavery of the African praise poets, the *Griots*, who used songs to their kings and others in the culture, and acted as folk historians.

As praise poets, the duB-poets were journalistic spokespersons for the common folk, and spoke up about news events in the history of the culture they lived in, giving praise or curse accordingly.

Nowadays, a derivative of the griot-style, rap, is commonplace, but most commonly, with the political stance not always there, the rappers boasting, or talking grandly of themselves...

Dub-poetry dealing with the politics of personal relationships is not too common, and is the essential feature of T-site. I have taken some of the rhythms too, away from much of their traditional bases and into the classical genre...

Sexuality/sensuality is one of the themes of T-site duB-poetry, and one of links and lens to understanding in an attempt to show how I believe it to be central in all our lives...

The poetry/music is a bare allegory of several world myth, a text based on the narrative of another text. The form/content is "mythic", following my theory of mathematics, especially regarding mythic discourses...

The images in the text are complex, especially as I don't always use simple metaphors, or anaematopia, but often construct a phrase or sentence so the meanings 'explode' in clusters and intentionally there must be several interpretations. This is a latter day influence on my poetry coming from French aesthetic theory. I do this to allow the reader to *write* meanings into the text; also have a choice of meaning, so that I as writer, and she/he are jointly constructing relationships: that is, *working* with words/music to produce a text. This is analogous to an element of free will...

Furthermore, no longer influenced by the Imagists and Hans Magnus Enzensberger, I now believe that images must be *startling*! and a worthwhile text must be struggled with, and enjoyed again and again; as well as being 'written' too by the reader.

Thus, a lot of my images exists as French critic Roland Barthes explains, as *elisons* : meanings that you can just understand as a reader, and when held in the mind, they 'slip' and you have to work to make them plain...

Too, there is a construct around a time base of eternity: the eternal-forever-now....

8. Egyptology

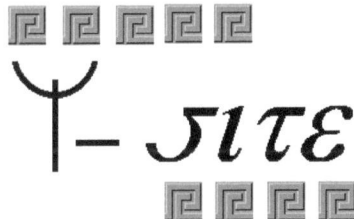

Analysis of T-site website logo

◩ = utter of river = ma/pa/daughter/son = all = heiroglyphics for "Egypt"...

◩ ◩ ◩ ◩ ◩ = ◩◩◩◩◩ = Egypt of Upper Nile...

◩ ◩ ◩ ◩ = ◩◩◩◩ = Egypt of Lower Nile...

Both together = community = people...

"T" = ankh = eye of logos/law = a signifier for Thoth = "Nature's Laws"... "Life"...

"-" = the River... Osiris, flooded...

U, l = Sun Ra, and - = River Thoth/nU = Laws of Life/Nature... Osiris living...

"site" ~ sight : "cite" = "saith" = "spoken way", or "myth"...

since Chaos = nU...

and T-site = sighted laws of the Ra River... A way of Osiris...

and there is a community...

All "word" = *"a written laws of life of the kingdom (heaven) of the river people"*...

All other wording outside the logo links Jah-aIe ~ Stanley Alexander Martin : his work on *Too* myth...
which is, to say:

"jaH-aYe's truth"... Stanley Alexander Martin's nature....

Part One
Prologue:
The Premonition of Death
(or, The Mass of the Dead)

Osiris Ra is dead, and his Life Nature is flooded, and is created Heaven; his wife Isis is beloving his re-created body; at the limit of eternity, Ra is knowing his son Horus, and the war of retribution to come with Seth, the slayer...

I.   Kyrie: Fell/risen

June, Osiris, so soon to risen flood...

was speaks of the spring ills,
the grey boy of summer:

held the ancient wisdom
in those two hands,
those mirroring two palms:

the rivers of his veins
pumped blood enough at
        nineteen to full
                the Atlantic Ocean:

before the Dead Kiss...

"I am the becoming," he said
        to the cry of dapper downs...
"I am the fling to far horizons!"
        to the city in trafficking streets...

...Am the infant
        suckling in interior streams,
am the child
        playing among troubled waters:
am the teenager
        ganging to liquid heaven...

"Am is the gathering-to of storms:
        the lion of summer
                is my thunder:
is my flash the kick of lightning;
I, a cumulus of clouds;
I, the eyelids of the rain...

With the Flood is the Promise
        of beside you
        besides, too

besides
a she and a himself
with the Flood came the opening doors to rain...

...He speaks of the spring ills,
the grey boy of summer:

held the ancient wisdom
in these two hands,
these mirroring two palms:

...He speaks
       and the owl of discontent
rises in the swaying wind;

"I am the becoming." he says
       to the wolf at the gulf moon
"I am the fling to far horizons!"
to the rush-hour passenger-in-passing...

...With the Flood comes the Promise
       of mating two
       beside you,
       besides
       a tight round collar
gives a blessing
       with the pain...

...Am his clinging
       rollercoast to your toast
       wringing to your waist
       two rims held in my two hands
a-falling to your call in me:
       virgin is the day becoming night....

With the schooling cane
the hurt of ruler:

a white chalk on black-bored;
a task of never was the tale tolled:

with the pains of thirteen asks around the sun,
cane the spots of scar-let-pimple-nick-elle,

the short daze of spring
let in the ills and downs of summer:

was never too proud the ruler of his class
to rule his heart:

with all the schooling to the mourning of this day
the morning sun was the nevers too bright to stare down his own gaze....

shall with the come the evening sun
the throws of winter's rage
the age of summer-through
-autumn, to December years:
the outburst of my passion shall
the supper tip no wine into
       your mother's milk:

I shall fine ale and repast
look the forward to
break-fast, and
no more till tomorrows...

till the glad tide-ins of the sun:

I moon at mine the future death....

...A bird torn from feathers
kites my clinging to sky back to cords;
same chords ringing in me the choir
same wring, the hands holding me from heaven...

II.   Gloria: Cursed/praised

...I am not worthy of female love
the crow of cock at dawn denies the hen:

would to a sleep beyond breakfasting:
I am the comings to a stiffer death...

...I am not the worthy of female love
she is holy flesh, wholier than I...

all things the sat on heaven...

...I know, I am not the worthy of femaled love
Another has vanquished me...

a spark out-pours the eternity of blythe the knowing of this
                                        and all other times the now...

...I am the river Death of night and day...
...the River's flood will the sap to a Child the Life...

awe! Or-us!...

III. Credo: Dismissed

Beg You
        forgive the Child the rich in spirit
                award them the heaven...
I beg You....

Beg You
        forgive the Child the never mourns
                comfort them in heaven...
I beg You....

Beg You
        forgive the Child the assertive
                let them inherit Nature...
I beg You....

Beg You
        forgive the Child the always righteous
                the spark with sap...
I beg You....

Beg You
        forgive the Child the un-merciful
                thank them with righteousness...
I beg You....

Beg You
        forgive the Child the jihad
                let them be gOd's children...
I beg You....

Beg You
        forgive the Child the persecute for righteousness
                let them inherit heaven...
I beg You....

Beg You
        forgive the Child the true voices:

rejoice them with the knowing the blythe of heaven...
        for they are the being The Children of the Time...
I beg You to the leave...

IV.   Sanctus: returns the made sacred/profane

October deep...

...if the deep...

...if the deep inside your Nature,
and that the Child is
nevers the sleep and
awakes to a high tide...

if the harvest of September...
the gathering to of crops,
if then the slow rise:

the Flood shall be planted anew...

light day shall be a beckon to
 the dark night beyond this life...

... We shall the journey into Heaven

V.   Benedictus: blessed/turned

Harvested the flood:
Eat!

...Of me the sweet juices of the fruit to wine...

...of me the biscuits...

Of me the living life!

Of me is made concrete...

I am real....

VI.   Agnus Dei: Sacrificed

May I cross over the light day plains:
I wither...

He came and kissed me
one sword and. here:

witness, I withered...

I crossed over the light day planes...

There *is* a God!

I die...

Go now....

...I come again!

3: Part Two   The Plagues
-Naked in asylum-
(after
Freud
Adler
Buber
Jung
Chomsky
Stack Sullivan
Lacan
Laing
Derrida)

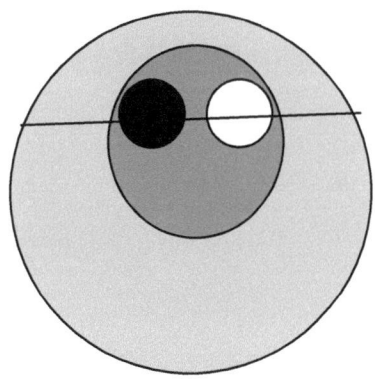

In the asylum, the incarnated Osiris is transcending into knowing his Ra Nature....
The wars with Seth begins…..

I.   dis-Equilibrium

Nineteen

i.

....The deepest night of day,
I am a storm;

a naked me
in a tidy hat...

I am a storm...

a flood to this
day tasking...

I am a storm...

ii.

Dawn to
your down/text textures...

I am morning
beloving
out the night:

as evers
the day, becalm
upon the shores
of this:

incident to
a myth...

dawn to
your down
day clusters...

the morning sun rose
as the dark night melts:
I am truly the winter nows
with/out
the sage of season, but
garnished with the light,
deferral to
a now-past
mine soul is
knowing
a have....

I am the awakening to
a happenstance....

iii.

Hold fast
those tremors of the brain:
child,
the soul is gifted dead
comes a living
beyond all other dreams
    the drama of that life:
        this life is gone...

...comes the woken
Spirits of the God:
the Voices of the Word:
comes a living man:
    this life is gone...

...as/to Another's:
the praises of the flesh
are worthless: now
    praises you Him!
and be care full:
all things will uncanny:

*an aweful way
your Path has trod:
the Persons of this
                Life
are Ghosts...*

*will be
a rainbow beyond the Flood...*

*ever be
        the speakings to of yourself....*

iv.

*Hold fast
child,
that hatred of
the Ghost:
Seth is Satan-you-in-yours
self: brother/essential gOd:*

*fear you
the doings of
yourself;
the makings of
yourself:
O, you must complete
the act of you...*

*...all things the living
have in theirs
completeness:
an essential nemesis
unique
in theirs the likeness...*

*...die/and theirs death
live and at odds, to
too conquer death:
know...*

...all pain is you...

v.

A cry to your
down
      day clusters

I am mourning
out
      the beloving of
a sun:

a yell
to this day
break-fast-into noon,

a storm
on the horizon of
all my yesterdays:

tomorrows heeds an ebb
to flood...

Shall she come....

vi.

Busy-bud to rain?

and so in winter?

I am here
and high above your
distemper:

smiling in your light-shine
welcomes the sunshine

heres a little
kissed upon yours
eyes....

vii.

Ah!...

am in
        another's world...

where am?

theirs eyes
are insights to
        theirs the soul

nine eyes:
green is devoted
blue is sexual
violet looketh upon me beloved
                      as gOd:
red is dreadful;
orange is just:

mine eyes showeth mine own

disorder...

small eyes criticise
big eyes show temperance...

"I"....

viii.

As she did come
and did the kiss me back;
I did sit into her lap,
and hugged among the high dales:

cream in her cushion cup:

the tides and storms will ebb
for us:

I will the do me well....

II.   Search

i.

A picket in his eyes
a shovel in his mouth
a pocket in his ears

this tall is
       the Pharoah...

"Chief Priest!"
the inmates
care full
gathering roundf about the me...

he's the one
decides on our doings;
our rations:
Head of the Mental State
ours building
a monument to his:

whenever
      I speak:
"hmm!"
they listen:
I: freed man among
slaves:
this time spent in mental labour:
the want is
      to usher in
           a holiday....

ii.

For you shall the love gOd

      I'm awake and far from home

                        on a windy eve in March...
I shall waste him:
this harang about
        my temple;
no peace:

I awake up,
he wakes
and begins the haunting;

I asleep,
he sits astride
the mares of night...

...the days are longer;
the River knows an ebb:

I tell them:

"Let my people breathe..."

and all in an asking to nU
I hate and I switch off a light:

for a week there is darkness!

...I would be rid of him!
that derringer in me...

...and somehow,
        deep inside,
an infant child is being
beloving....

iii.

**For you shall the love
        the neighbouring me...**

            I'm aware and far from rest

on a windy eve in March...

I shall waste him:
this harang about
      my temple;
no peace:

I awake up,
he wakes
and begins the haunting;

I asleep,
he sits astride
the mares of night...

...the days are longer;
the River knows an ebb:

I tell them:

"Let my people breathe..."

and all in an asking to nU
I weep at a torment:

for a week there is rain!

...I would be rid of him!
that derringer in me...

...and somehow,
      deep inside,
an infant child is being
beloving....

iv.

Shall she relate fair

I'm the connected to you
               on a windy eve in March...

I shall waste him:
this harang about
          my temple;
no peace:

I awake up,
he wakes
and begins the haunting;

I asleep,
he sits astride
the mares of night...

...the days are longer;
the River knows an ebb:

I tell them:

"Let my people breathe..."

and all in an asking to nU
I vomit up a meal:

for a week there is an infestation of flies!

...I would be rid of him!
that derringer in me...

...and somehow,
          deep inside,
an infant child is being
beloving....

v.

Shall she learn skilled

>   I'm linked into you
>   on a windy eve in March...

I shall waste him:
this harang about
         my temple;
no peace:

I awake up,
he wakes
and begins the haunting;

I asleep,
he sits astride
the mares of night...

...the days are longer;
the River knows an ebb:

I tell them:

"Let my people breathe..."

and all in an asking to nU
I bleed from a wound:

for a week all hear Spirits!

...I would be rid of him!
that derringer in me...

...and somehow,
         deep inside,
an infant child is being
beloving....

vi.

Shall she play live

        I'm the knowing you
              the storm a windy eve in March...

I shall waste him:
this harang about
    my temple;
no peace:

I awake up,
he wakes
and begins the haunting;

I asleep,
he sits astride
the mares of night...

...the days are longer;
the River knows an ebb:

I tell them:

"Let my people breathe..."

and all in an asking to nU
I climb a stair:

We begin the ascent into Heaven!

...I am the begin to be rid of him!
that derringer in me...

...and somehow,
    deep inside,
an infant child is
beloving....

                              the storm
subsides in April
                    the storm subsides
  in April...

              the storm the begin to subside in April...

III.   Meeting on the River

Once upon a time:
    I was
To honeymoon with you,
      And
I awoke to hear
The toll of bells....

Y'know,
Madness is such a lonely
      Room,
I want to always
Be where you are:
    But
Now you're here
    I
Watch the blossoming smile:
    I
Glimpse the dimple
In your cheek,
   I hold tight on
Your hand:
You must never go away....

And now you say
    It's
A holy day:
    You've come
To take me home....

I
Wondered why it didn't
Rain all day....
....You've come to take me home....

I shall see you every day....

Where was the hell
     That tore my heart:

"you wouldn't come after all"….
But now you're here
          You're here now
                    You're here now…..

                              You're here….

3. Exodus to Being

Osiris Ra is the found and begun the beloving by Isis….
They exodus from Shenley Hospital by bus along the Radlett Road and then by train to Acton…..

I.   The RADLETT ROAD

The sun a shining…
The day is dark….
My sky is a climbing…
          Climbing…
Tomorrow's a see

I'm the rising
Rising….

Up and above the ocean….
Too to two….
A monster the feel of flight….

Ra is ascendant…
Heaven…
Heaven….

The sun is shining
My sky is clear
Haven…
Haven….

I'd rather this time she had chinese eyes…..

Do I love your frock?
Zen!

Do I love your tiers?….

Do I love your chinese eyes?

I'll give you a house!
I'll give you a child!

Ra is ascended!
Ra is ascended!
Ra is ascended!

Could you please come to me
The
Zen
Way…..

Back to a beach….

Jah is descended….

Rather….

I'll
Find us a home….

Ra is descended

I'll find us a home….

Jah is ascended….

Ra is descended….
Jah is ascended….
Ra is descended….
Jah is ascended….

Zhan!…..

Come kiss me with the smiles of your lips
My love has a chinese mouth….

You take away the nights!
My love has a chinese mouth….

You're the secret I can't keep
My love has an ancient mind…..

Owhl!
Love has a chinese kiss….

You take away the day!

Love has a chinese kiss!….

You sleep within mon soeur
Love has a chinese kiss!

You're more heaven when heaven wans….
Love has a chinese kiss….

You try to take away my hands….
Love has a chinese kiss
You try to take away my legs….
Love has a chinese kiss…
You're heaven when heaven wans….
Love has a chinese kiss…

Ahh! The night of all other nights….
Heaven has the chinese eyes…..

Far on another day
Besides the tide of olden time
You and I in bliss
Me proud
And you the she-line/that
I never fail to blush….

Fun on a <u>key</u> day
Fun on a key day…..

A smile line
      And a love line sometimes….

Shall I the tell you

June and the solstice….
A flood in my happy day….
The moon has the risen on me….
A smile on a happy day….
She's moonshine….
A smile on a happy day
Smile on a happy day….

The River is flooded….
Smile on a happy day….
The River is flooded….
Smile on a happy day…..

I shall the rise the bidden dawn….
I shall rise the ridden sky….
June and the solstice
Rise the ridden dawn….

Isis is ascended….

Flood the ridden dawn….

Isis is ascended….

Horus is awakening….

Flood the risen dawn….

Horus is awakening….

Flood the risen dawn…..

Dark-night-sometimes
Wears the ring of the sun sunrays….
Some of the moon's shine
Summers her sometimes
With a night
The day-like robes
The darkness fells
Robbery of day with sunshine…..

Back to begin….

The sun a shining….
The day is dark!
My sky is a climbing
            Climbing….

Tomorrow's a see….

I'm the rising
Rising….
To above the ocean….

Horus must be born!
He's a beautiful son…
He's looking back at me….
He's a beautiful son!
He's looking back here at me….

And I'm storming down the Radlett Road with you!
With you
With you…..

II.   RADLETT to St. PANCRAS

My dark night sometimes
Wears the moon's daylights;
Some of her shine
Summers me sometimes
With bright
The day-likes robs:
The darkness tells
Robbery of sunshine
When the dawn of morning wells….

It's vehicle of a wars
My hate-She to hate-Him, my Hates,
And now He's peace
My Perfection in Perhaps
Within cite:
The shine of wrath robes:
My darkness the fells
A robber of sunshine
And sent Him back to His hells…..

III. St. PANCRAS to KING'S CROSS - The split Red Sea

i.

I awake in morning,
         and
a kiss come unto
         the me....
the contour/colour of your face....

Redeem
       the rhythm of
            the day:
come night onto
           the day,

the rising sun come onto
            the day:
the morning of
           the day....

Shall say:
       the sun shine
       shineth
       shineth for all

shall say:
       night onto

       the saying,
       sayeth
in the rhythm of the day
       the sun shineth
       for All
       the morning come
       the day

shall I

                        the awake
in mornings, and
            comes a kiss
            come unto me:
            come....

the colour to the contour of
                your face:

shall U the saying
                "the day comes
                come the day:
                come
the shining to the day
this morning of the day:

a colour come to
            the contour of
                    my face...."

"Come!"

ii.

I shall the roam your River....
            And cross the split Red Sea....

I shall the tender you tribute
            And cross the split Red Sea...

For you are Another's...
            And I am the grateful...

For you are another's
            And I am the great full...

...I-sis, I'm rowing up your route
            crossing the split Red Sea...

Shall a sail or put on board

        crossing your split Red sea...

I shall the roam your River....
        And cross the split Red Sea....

I shall the tender you tribute
        And cross the split Red Sea...

For you are Another's...
        And I am the grateful...

For you are another's
        And I am the great full...

...I-sis, I'm rowing up your route
        crossing the split Red Sea...

SO NEAR THE PROMISED LAND!....

IV.   KING'S CROSS to ACTON TOWN

i.

The run in-day,
I,
      a running day:

the run in-day:

come...

This burden
    is
      the heavy is
      is the heavy is
      is the heavy
          is....

comes to in-day
      come to
the run-way,
      comes to
the run-in day....

"Thank you!"

ii.

"I",
      the seat in day
      seeth in-day....

"We" are on a train....

"I",
      come mornings to the sun
         come to
         with night:

a passenger to this day....

"heaven" is
        El....

"sHe" is Heaven
        "I",
                hell....
comes to a dawning come to
                      come to

the rising of the sun:

"You the crying...."

I weep no more....

"You the crying?"

"Weep no more..."

iii.

He give me
        a garland for
                my eyes:

your face:
        a Garden for
        my eyes....

you the gift me
        a Garden for my eyes....

Can I stand
        the live-ins
        without
        you?

iv.

Give me
> a garden
> for my eyes:

I am
> a Garden
> for the eyes:

the sun
> the gathers to a
> > shine....

v.

The shine you....

"I",
> the naked unto:

the shame you:
> **"I"....**

the naked unto?

Shame you?

"I spoke!"...

am the speaking!

Spoke!

vi.

It's a
> **beautiful?**

"I the
> **spoken**

speaks...."

It's a beautiful?....

"One!"

"Why am I the beautiful?"

I the naked unto
 You?

vii.

*"Am I naked
 unto You?"*

sHe
the speak in
 riddles:

**Shall I
 the speak too?**

She is
the speaking to
spoke in
riddles...

**"Am I
 the speaking to?"**

*"Yes,
 I spoke!"*

"Yes....

"I "spoke" too!"

"I spoke too!

"For the first time!"

"We riseth!"

V. ACTON TOWN - The Five Commandments

i.

Do we
>   needeth
>   the fly away....

Together....

ii.

Is spoken to....

"The sun
>   shineth for All!"

"Does the Sun "shine"?"

"Shineth...."

"For All?"....

iii.

"Is spoken to...."

Truly?

"No!"

Is the spoken to?

I shall speak!

*"The spoken
>   to!"*

"ale!"

"aYe...."

iv.

Shall she the love gOd

    I'm awake and home
        on a stormy night in June...

Shall she the love
*   the neighbouring me...*

    I'm aware at rest
        on a stormy night in June...

Shall she relate fair

    I'm the connected to you
        on a stormy night in June...

Shall she learn skilled

    I'm linked into you
        on a stormy night in June...

Shall she play live

    I'm the knowing you
        the storm a night in June...

    the storm
a night in June...

    the storm a-night
  in June...

    the storm a night in the midst of June...

5. The Promised Land

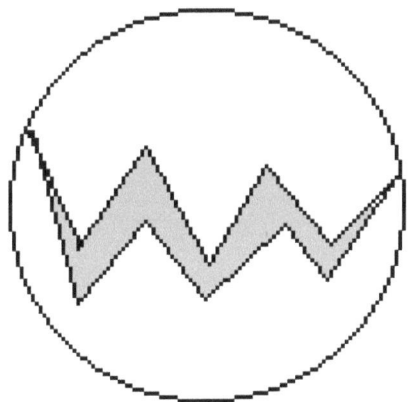

The River is flooded....
Osiris Ra and Isis belove into the birth of Horus....
Osiris Ra ascends finally into Heaven…..

I.   Promised

...Spoken of
       the choir-at
             a

child in
    a
Big man

aNubis,
      the fill?

"I, and
      aNada?

and,
      too,
           Horus..."

arriver?

"Too,
      then...

then...
      Horus...."

ii.

Night drips in dusk
      nice as my pen-nib swells
as spoke into the sponge of paper sucks,
      nibbles into ink wells
the writing tells
      of night hung on a moon at tusk.

Dark-night-sometimes
      wears sometime-yellow rags
some of the moon's shine summers her sometimes

>   with gold the sun day robs,
> the golden flags
>   love-looks at summer's-day-sometimes
> love-looks at summer;s day sometimes...
>
> And night warming
>   as moon captures sun ways
> rays striptease into naked returning
>   night into blushes blaze,
> moon's wax waylays
>   dawn drizzling day - oh!: morning!
> morning...

iii.

If I was your kind-and-country
cook-into-olive-oil,
would the pot make the pigeon broil
would your taste take a fancy
more than the one time?
-fiancee?

If you were your lady-looking
-milk-made-and-marriage-maid,
would the Prince put you on parade
would you think me good-looking
once more than sometimes?
-your boyfriend?

If I was your holy-worship
-woman-with-given-Spark-
would you desire me as your Ark
would you come to my service
once and for all time?
-wouldst love me?

iv.

Should tongue diet
live a voice fasting self?
food is what the mouth wants on the quiet
put hunger on the shelf
one loves oneself:
put fire and finger into fat!

Whose shame say 'can'ts'?
fat is to taste of Love
flesh is what the cake-and-cherry-world wants
life has so little of,
do what size does
and shame those who devil us: 'can'ts'.

Eat and let live
make the taste-buds riot
pork give, give bacon, make the stomach give
don't give-in to diet:
since man eats fat
why so you think that repulsive?
        why so you think that repulsive?....

v.

Was I your hug-and-apple-pie
sink-into-an-apron,
would my strings be your scaffold strung
my smile there to make you try
would you love always?
-live in me?

And if I your payfling-and-fight
rival-soldier-in-arms,
would I to doll to pick up charms
be chubby your little light
yours always always?
-inside me?

*If I was your gold-and-wed-ring
kiss-on-to-cushion-him,
would I just wearer of purse string
stranger-loved with whom lived-in:
one's lover always?
-love you me?*

vi.

Love or life dies
    live mouth against a kiss
even if the stars fall hearts shall shout skies
    sun in shine shall be bliss
hail-storm amiss
    won't warry weather with the windrush rise

and conquer this:
    love is but bare second
a moment in a turning round to kiss
    shall a finger beckon
love to reckon,
    dues paid for such credited blythe.
dues paid for such credited blythe...

Heed thus on end
    how silenced heart is free
how stone open-heart surgery can mend:
    can stained heart welcome me
your lover be
    your love-friend more than your boyfriend?
your love-friend more than your boyfriend?

vii.

If I was your all-out-war-friend
brother-in-law-in-arms,
would you stick to me through these storms
would our love come to an end
would you kill so still?
-and in love?

If I was your union-at-work
comrade-in-uniform,
would you rally to me each morn
strike a light even though broke
would you weary still?

-friend and love?

If I was your carpenter's mate
married-man-to-the-wood,
would you share with me bread and blood
or tinder me your ungrate
would you cross so still?
-and beloved?....

-and beloved?....

-and beloved?....

-and beloved?....

-AND, be loved?....

II. Land

i.

I fly/I fly
I say…
I fly/I fly….

And….

I'm not the bird in flight…..
I fly/I fly
I say…
I fly/I fly….

And
I'm not the bird in flight…..

Shall I the shall I?

Shall I the surrenderings to my flight:
       I fly:
         Shall I the surrender to my flight….

I fly….
And….

The day is a bliss to night!…..

ii.

O! I've
Been raised through
Hell and high water….

Run with the River:
    Heard my inner voices:
Met with the Lord…..

If the sleep….

      And the sleep/comes
Inner dream….
If the sleep/and dream….
And the dream an inner bliss

I rest
I rest….

Been too
The Roaring Silence….
And: all my tears have dried
And all my wasted years
From a wasteland
      Turned, a wilderness of grass…..

If the sleep….
      And the sleep/comes
Inner dream….
If the sleep/and dream….
And the dream an inner bliss

I rest
I rest….

Exit….

Into Heaven….

Exit into Heaven…..

…pTaH-aYe…..
…..
…..
…iOttOi-aYe…..
….*IoTToI-Ra*…..

Stanley Alexander MARTIN/Nana baBa jaH-aYe
Rainham, KENT,
11:24 am British Summer Time 30 July 2007

www.ingramcontent.com/pod-product-compliance
Ingram Content Group UK Ltd.
Pitfield, Milton Keynes, MK11 3LW, UK
UKHW041434180426
11947UKWH00007B/444